Kindness Counts!

D0106673

Ready, Freddy!

2nd Grade

Kindness Counts!

by ABBY KLEIN

illustrated by
JOHN McKINLEY

Scholastic Inc.

To My Mother:
You inspired me every day with your genuine
caring for other people, and you taught me
that kindness really does count!
Love you forever...
xo,
Me

Text copyright © 2018 by Abby Klein

Illustrations copyright © 2018 by John McKinley

All rights reserved. Published by Scholastic Inc., *Publishers since 1920.*
SCHOLASTIC and associated logos are trademarks and/or registered
trademarks of Scholastic Inc.

The publisher does not have any control over and does not assume
any responsibility for author or third-party websites or their content.

No part of this publication may be reproduced, stored in a retrieval
system, or transmitted in any form or by any means, electronic,
mechanical, photocopying, recording, or otherwise, without written
permission of the publisher. For information regarding permission,
write to Scholastic Inc., Attention: Permissions Department,
557 Broadway, New York, NY 10012.

This book is a work of fiction. Names, characters, places, and incidents
are either the product of the author's imagination or are used
fictitiously, and any resemblance to actual persons, living or dead,
business establishments, events, or locales is entirely coincidental.

ISBN 978-1-338-28135-4

11 10   22 23

Printed in the U.S.A.   40

First printing 2018

Book design by Mary Claire Cruz

CHAPTERS

I have a problem. A really, really big problem. It's Random Acts of Kindness Week at my school. All week we are going to be doing kind things at school, at home, and in our community. In my class we are also going to pick names out of a hat, and we have to do something kind for the person we pick. What if I pick Max, the biggest bully in the whole second grade? He is never kind to anyone.

What am I going to do?

CHAPTER 1

RAKs

The bus pulled up in front of school, and I jumped off. "See you at recess!" I yelled over my shoulder to my best friend Robbie.

"Meet you by the big tree!" he yelled back.

As I walked down the hall toward my room, I saw my teacher, Miss Clark, come around the corner, carrying a huge pile of books. There must have been about twenty books in the stack, and she was moving very slowly, trying not to drop them.

I ran up to her. "Good morning, Miss Clark."

She carefully peeked around the stack of books in her arms. "Oh, good morning, Freddy. I thought that was you, but it's hard to see over all these books!" she said with a chuckle.

"Let me help you carry some of those," I said, pointing to the stack. "I wouldn't want you to drop them."

"That's so nice of you," said Miss Clark. "My arms are getting a little tired. I've had to carry these all the way from the library."

Miss Clark bent down slightly. "Why don't you take some off the top, Freddy," she said.

I reached up and carefully took some books off the top of the stack.

"Whew! That's a lot better," said Miss Clark. "You are so sweet for offering to help."

I smiled. "No problem," I said. "What are all these books for?"

"Well, we are starting our nonfiction writing unit," said Miss Clark. "I thought it would be fun if everyone did some nonfiction writing about their favorite animal, so I checked out a bunch of animal books from the library."

"Cool! I know which animal I'm going to write about," I said.

"Let me guess," said Miss Clark. "Sharks!"

I laughed. "Yep! Sharks are my favorite animal in the whole wide world! I love learning about them and—"

All of a sudden, someone bumped into me with their backpack and almost sent me flying to the ground. I caught myself just in time and looked up. Of course it was Max, the biggest bully in the whole second grade.

He was chasing Chloe down the hall, and she was waving her arms in the air and screaming, "Help! Help! Someone help me!"

Max just laughed and ran faster without watching where he was going. He accidentally crashed right into Miss Clark, and all the books she was carrying flew out of her hands and hit the ground with a *thud*.

Max froze. He stared at Miss Clark.

"Max," she said. "How many times have I told you not to run in the hallway? Now look what just happened because you weren't following the school rules."

Max remained frozen like a statue. "I . . . I . . . I . . . ummm . . . ," he stammered.

"How about saying you're sorry?" asked Miss Clark.

"I'm sorry," Max mumbled.

"Now you can help me pick up all the books."

"I already did that," Jessie said.

Miss Clark turned around and there was Jessie, holding all the books that Max had knocked to the ground.

"Jessie, that was so kind of you to pick up all these books," said Miss Clark. "I really appreciate that."

"Any time," Jessie said with a smile. "I'm always happy to help."

We all walked into the classroom and put our things away.

"I need everyone to come over to the rug," said Miss Clark. "We have something we need to talk about."

"We need to talk about how Max is such a big meanie," Chloe said as she made her way over to the rug.

"I am not!" Max barked in Chloe's face.

"You are, too! A big, giant meanie," Chloe said, sticking her tongue out at Max.

"All right. That's enough, you two," said Miss Clark. "You both need to stop yelling at each other and sit down on the rug. Chloe, you sit here, and Max, you sit over there."

"Yeah. As far away from each other as possible," I whispered to Josh.

"First of all," said Miss Clark, "what just happened out there is a good reminder of why we don't run in the hallway. If you're running, then you're not watching where you are going, and you can easily bump into people."

"But I had to run," Chloe whined. "Max was chasing me."

"Max and Chloe, remember our school rule is you must walk in the hallways," said Miss Clark.

Chloe crossed her arms, stuck out her lower lip, and pouted.

"This morning's incident was also a good example of something else," Miss Clark continued.

"Really? What?" asked Jessie.

"It was a good example of what I call RAKs," said Miss Clark.

"RAKs? What are those?" asked Josh.

"R-A-K stands for Random Acts of Kindness."

"What does that mean?" said Jessie.

"It means doing something kind for someone when they aren't expecting it," said Miss Clark. "This morning two people in our class performed random acts of kindness. First, Freddy offered to help me carry my huge stack of books, and then Jessie helped me pick them up when they went flying all over the place."

"Oh, I get it," said Jessie.

"Kindness is contagious," said Miss Clark.

"EEEWWWWW!" said Chloe. "You mean it spreads germs?"

"No," said Miss Clark. "I mean when we do kind things for people, they feel so good about what we did that they want to do kind things for other people."

"So the kindness is passed on and on to a lot of people," said Josh.

"Exactly," said Miss Clark. "And Mr. Pendergast has decided that we are going to have a Random Acts of Kindness Week here at school."

"That's cool," I said.

"All week you will look for ways to show other people you care," said Miss Clark. "Every time you perform a random act of kindness, either at school, at home, or in our community, then you are going to write what you did on a strip of paper like this and attach it to our school Kindness Chain. We are going to see if

we can make a chain that goes around the whole school by the end of the week."

"Wow! That sounds awesome!" said Jessie. "I can already think of a million things I can do for other people."

"Wonderful," said Miss Clark. "But to make sure that each person does at least one kind act this week, I put everyone's name in a hat, and whoever's name you pick, you have to perform one random act of kindness for that person sometime this week."

"Watch me pick Max's name out of the hat," I whispered to Josh. "Whenever we do something like this, I always end up with Max."

"Maybe you won't this time," whispered Josh. "You never know."

Miss Clark started walking around with the hat full of names. Kids picked a name out one at a time. My heart was pounding in my chest. *Please don't let me pick Max*, I thought to myself. *Please, please, please.*

Miss Clark finally got to me. I closed my eyes

and reached my hand in the hat. I swirled the papers around and pulled one out. I opened one eye, then the other. Then I slowly opened the piece of paper. My heart sank.

"I got Jessie," Josh whispered excitedly. "Who did you get?"

I couldn't even speak. I just turned and held up the slip of paper in front of Josh's nose. Printed on the paper were three letters . . . M-A-X.

CHAPTER 2

Amazing Ideas

"Told you so," I whispered to Josh. "I knew it! I just knew it! I knew I was going to pick Max's name . . . just like when we did Secret Santa. I'm always the one who gets stuck with Max. What am I going to do?"

"Don't worry, Freddy," said Josh. "You'll think of something."

"Easy for you to say. You're so lucky you picked Jessie. Of course I had to pick the biggest bully in the whole second grade!"

"Keep that name you picked a secret," Miss

Clark said, and smiled. "You want your random act of kindness for that person to be a surprise. Remember, we are going to be doing this all week."

I'm going to need that long to come up with something kind to do for Max, I thought to myself.

"Now," said Miss Clark. "Let's see if we can brainstorm some ideas of kind things you all can do throughout the week, so the Kindness Chain can make it all the way around our school. Does anyone have any ideas?"

Chloe waved her hand wildly in the air. "Me, me . . . me, me, me! I have lots of ideas!" she said. She jumped up and walked to the front of the room. "You're going to LOVE my ideas!"

"Sit down, Fancypants," said Max. "Miss Clark didn't call on you."

Chloe put her hands on her hips and glared at Max. "Oh yes she did."

"Oh no she didn't," Max shot back.

"Yes she did, and you're not the boss of me, so you can't tell me what to do," Chloe whined, and stamped her foot.

Miss Clark shook her head and mumbled, "Here we go again."

Max jumped up and started to walk toward Chloe. Miss Clark gently put her hand on his shoulder and directed him back to his spot on the rug.

"But . . . but . . . ," Max protested, "she's not the boss."

"I know," said Miss Clark, smiling. "I am."

Chloe frowned and stuck out her lower lip.

"Now, Chloe, please sit back down on the rug. We'd love to hear your ideas, but you have to wait until I have called on you. Just because you raise your hand doesn't mean you get to go first."

Chloe stuck her lower lip out even farther, hung her head, and slowly shuffled back to her seat.

"Look at her," whispered Jessie. "She is such a drama queen."

"Now, where were we . . . ?" said Miss Clark.

"You wanted some ideas of random acts of kindness," said Jessie.

"Oh, right. Thanks, Jessie," said Miss Clark. "Do you have any ideas of kind acts you could do here at school?"

Jessie smiled. "I do."

"Great! We would love to hear them."

Chloe folded her arms across her chest and sighed heavily.

"I have two ideas," said Jessie. "You could play with someone new at recess, and you could clean up someone else's mess at snack time."

"Those are two wonderful ideas," said Miss Clark. "Does anyone else have a suggestion?"

Miss Clark called on Josh. "If you're waiting for a turn on the swings at recess, you could let someone go in front of you," said Josh.

"What?" Max blurted out. "That's crazy! Why would I let someone cut in front of me?"

"Because that's a kind thing to do," said Miss Clark. "That's what this week is all about. Thinking about other people and showing them that you care."

Josh elbowed me in the side. "Get a load of Max's face right now," he whispered. "He looks very confused."

"That's because I don't think he knows what the word 'caring' means," I whispered back.

Josh laughed.

"How about at home?" Miss Clark asked. "What kind acts could you do for your family?"

Chloe's hand shot up and she bounced up and down, but she didn't yell out, so Miss Clark called on her.

"You could buy everyone in your family really expensive gifts! I could get my mom this fancy gold ring she saw at the jewelry store in the mall yesterday, and I could get my dad one

24

of those huge television sets that takes up a whole wall, and—"

Miss Clark cut her off. "Giving presents to people you love is a thoughtful thing to do, but that is not what this week is about."

"What do you mean?" said Chloe, scrunching up her nose.

I elbowed Josh this time. "Get a load of Chloe's face right now," I whispered. "Now she's the one who looks confused."

"That's because I don't think she knows how to make someone happy without spending money," Josh whispered back.

"You got that right." I chuckled.

"What I mean is that you want to think about what someone else might need and then offer your help," said Miss Clark. "Random Acts of Kindness Week is about helping other people with our actions, not with our money."

Chloe still looked confused.

"Let's see if anyone else has any ideas about what you could do at home to help your family," said Miss Clark.

I raised my hand. "You could help fold the laundry or vacuum the carpets," I said.

"Super ideas!" said Miss Clark. "You want to come do that at my house, Freddy?"

I smiled. Chloe pouted.

Jessie raised her hand. "I could help my *abuela*, my grandma, wash the dishes after dinner, or take out the garbage."

"Garbage! Pee-yew!" Chloe said, holding her nose. "Garbage is stinky."

"Wow!" said Miss Clark, ignoring Chloe. "You all are coming up with some great ideas!"

"I have an idea of something you could do for your neighbor," said Josh. "The other day I saw that one of my neighbors has a lot of weeds in her garden. I could go pull out all the weeds."

"I could write a kind note and put it in my neighbor's mailbox," said Margo, another girl in my class.

"You all have definitely got some amazing ideas," said Miss Clark. "And I know that your caring and thoughtful acts of kindness will bring happiness to other people. Then they will pass that kindness on to someone else, and that person will pass it on to someone else, and on and on and on."

Just then I had a great idea. I raised my hand.

"Yes, Freddy," said Miss Clark.

"I have an idea of something we could do as a whole class," I said.

"Really? I'd love to hear it."

"We could all bring in one book that we don't read anymore and one toy that we don't play with anymore and donate them to the kids living in the homeless shelter."

A big smile spread across Miss Clark's face. "I love that idea, Freddy! What do you all think?" Miss Clark asked the rest of the class.

"I love it, too!" said Jessie.

"Me, too!" said Josh.

"Me, too! Me, too! Me, too!" everyone chimed in.

"Great!" said Miss Clark. "We'll do it. Look around your house and find one book and one toy to donate and bring them in to school by the end of the week. We'll collect them here in the classroom, and then I can bring them over to the homeless shelter this weekend."

Finding a book and toy to donate would be easy. Thinking of something kind to do for Max was going to be the hard part.

CHAPTER 3

Underwear War

All the way home on the bus, I tried to think of random acts of kindness I could do for my family. I had one good idea, but I wanted to surprise my mom.

"Mom! Mom!" I yelled as I opened the front door and ran into the house, dropping my backpack on the kitchen floor.

My mom was in the kitchen, talking on the phone. She pulled it away from her ear for a minute and whispered, "This is a very important call, Freddy. I just need a few more minutes."

"No problem," I mouthed, giving her a thumbs-up.

I slowly and quietly backed out of the kitchen and tiptoed toward the laundry room. Just as I opened the door—"UMPH!" I bumped right into my sister, Suzie.

"Hey, watch where you're going!" she growled.

"Why don't you watch where *you're* going," I snapped back. "What are you doing in here, anyway?"

"I could ask you the same question," said Suzie. "What does it look like I'm doing? I'm taking the laundry upstairs to fold it. It's going to be a random act of kindness for Mom. She's going to be so surprised."

"But I was going to do that as a random act of kindness," I said. "I planned the whole thing on the way home on the bus."

"Well, so did I," said Suzie, "and it looks like I beat you to it, so you'll just have to find something else to do."

"That's not fair," I whined. "I thought of it first."

"So what?"

"So I should get to do it."

"Sorry." Suzie grinned. "You were too slow, Joe. You know what they say, 'The last one there is a rotten egg,' so I guess you're a rotten egg," she said, holding her nose.

"But I really, really wanted to do it," I pleaded.

"What's it worth to you?" Suzie said, holding up her pinkie for a pinkie swear.

I sighed. "I don't know . . . how about you get to control the TV remote for the next two days."

"Two days? Are you kidding me?" Suzie said, laughing. "Make it three days, and we have a deal."

"Three days? Three days?! You're crazy."

Suzie waved her pinkie in my face. "Do we have a deal or not?" she said.

I really wanted to do this for my mom. "Fine!" I said. "We have a deal." I went to lock pinkies with Suzie to seal the deal, but she pulled her pinkie away.

"Hey! What are you doing?" I said. "I thought we had a deal."

"I changed my mind," said Suzie. "The deal is off."

"You can't do that," I said. "We already agreed on three days. I'm not giving you four."

"Calm down, Sharkbreath," said Suzie. "I have an idea."

"I don't want to hear your dumb idea."

"Oh really? I think you're going to want to hear it."

"Fine. What is it?" I said.

"Why don't we do it together?" said Suzie.

"Together? You mean, like, you and me?" I said, pointing to her and then pointing to myself.

"Yes, you and me, Freddy and Suzie."

"And what do you want from me?"

"Nothing," said Suzie.

"What do you mean 'nothing'?" I asked suspiciously.

"I mean nothing," Suzie repeated. "Nada. A big, fat zero."

"What's the catch?" I said.

"There is no catch," said Suzie. "Since this is Random Acts of Kindness Week, this is my first act of kindness. You can have something you want without having to make a deal with me."

"Wow! Thanks," I said, giving Suzie a hug.

"You're welcome," she said, grinning. "Now, let's get a move on. We need to get all these clothes folded before Mom gets off the phone!"

We each grabbed one end of the laundry basket and carried it upstairs to Suzie's room.

"You know Mom is a neat freak," said Suzie, "so make sure you fold everything VERY carefully. No wrinkles."

"Aye, aye, Captain," I said, saluting Suzie.

"Fold the shirts like this. Lay it down on the

floor. Fold in one side, and then the other.
Then fold it in half like this and run your hand
over it to smooth out any wrinkles. Got it?"

"Got it!" I said.

We got to work folding the shirts. When the
shirts were all finished, we moved on to pants
and shorts.

"Put the legs together," said Suzie. "Then fold
them in half and smooth out the wrinkles."

"Okeydokey," I said. "I think I've got the hang of it."

"We need to hurry," said Suzie. "I'm sure Mom will be off the phone any minute. What's left?"

I peered into the laundry basket. "Socks and . . . underwear!" I said as I tossed a pair of my dad's underwear in Suzie's direction. They landed on her head.

"Ha, ha, ha!" I laughed hysterically. "I love your hat."

"Very funny," Suzie said, picking up a pair of my mom's underwear and flinging it at me.

It landed on my head and hung down into my eye. "Hey, hey, hey!" I said. "This means war."

We both started grabbing underwear out of the laundry basket and throwing it at each other. Pretty soon we looked like two trees decorated for Christmas with underwear ornaments.

We looked at each other and burst out laughing. "Ha, ha, ha, ha, ha!"

Then Suzie froze, grabbed my arm, and put her finger to her lips. "Shhhhh," she said. "I think I hear Mom coming."

We both listened in silence for a minute. "Yes! It's her! It's her!" I said, scrambling to pull all the underwear off me and quickly fold it in half.

Her footsteps were getting closer and closer. She was now climbing the stairs. "Kids, where are you?" she called.

"Hurry!" said Suzie. "We just have the socks left."

We frantically matched up the socks to make pairs.

"Freddy, Suzie, I know you're up here. I'm off the phone now."

"We're in here, Mom," Suzie called from her bedroom, just as we finished matching up the last pair of socks.

"Phew!" I sighed, glancing over at Suzie and wiping my forehead. "We made it just in time."

My mom opened the door and peeked her head in the room. "What are you two doing in here?"

"Surprise!" we yelled.

My mom walked into the room and looked down on Suzie's bed. "Did you just fold all this laundry?"

We both nodded.

"Wow! What a great surprise! Thank you so much," my mom said, giving us each a hug.

"That was our first RAK," we said together.

"Your first what?" asked my mom.

"Our first RAK," said Suzie, grinning. "It's Random Acts of Kindness Week at school, and this was our first random act of kindness."

CHAPTER 4

More RAKs

The next morning when the bus arrived, I hopped on. "Good morning, Mr. Franklin," I said to our bus driver, and then I handed him a doughnut.

Mr. Franklin looked surprised. "What's this for?" he asked.

I smiled. "No special reason," I said. "Just because I think you're a great bus driver."

"Thank you so much, Freddy," said Mr. Franklin. "Chocolate-covered doughnuts are my favorite!"

"Mine, too!" I said, and laughed.

Mr. Franklin took a big bite. "And this chocolate doughnut is delicious!" he said, licking his lips. "You just brought a little sunshine into my day." He took another giant bite, and I went to go sit down.

As I was walking to my seat, I was so focused on my best friends, Robbie and Josh, that I didn't see Max stick his foot out into the aisle. I tripped over his foot and fell *splat* on the floor of the bus.

I looked up, and there was Max with a big grin on his face. "Hey, Freddy, did you have a nice trip?" he asked, laughing hysterically.

I was so embarrassed. I could feel my cheeks burning bright red. I scrambled to my feet and sat down next to Robbie and Josh.

"Are you okay, Freddy?" they asked.

"Yeah, I'm fine," I mumbled.

"I think he's a little confused," said Robbie. "He thinks it's RAM Week."

"RAM Week?" Josh and I asked, puzzled. "What's that?"

"Random Acts of Meanness!" Robbie said.

The three of us burst out laughing, "Ha, ha, ha, ha, ha!"

Max turned around in his seat and yelled, "Hey, wimps, what's so funny back there?"

We ignored him and kept laughing.

Max got up on his knees and raised his voice. "Maybe you babies didn't hear me," he said. *"What's so funny back there!?"*

Just then Mr. Franklin said, "Max, sit down in your seat and leave Freddy and his friends alone."

Before Max turned around, he glared at us and whispered just loud enough for us to hear, "This isn't over. Just wait until recess." Then he sat back down in his seat.

"Oh, great," I mumbled. "I get to spend another recess being chased by the biggest bully in the whole second grade."

"What's his problem?" said Robbie.

"I don't think he has a kind bone in his body," I said.

"If this really were Random Acts of Meanness Week," said Josh, "then Max could do enough unkind acts all by himself to make a Meanness Chain that would go around the whole school!"

"You got that right," agreed Robbie.

"And don't worry about recess, Freddy. I'll be with you, and you know Max backs down when I bring out my karate moves," Josh said, karate chopping the air.

Chloe happened to be sitting in the seat in front of us, and Josh's fingers accidentally got caught in her hair.

"OW! OOOWWWW!" Chloe screamed, trying to yank her head away. "You're pulling my hair! You're pulling my hair!"

"It was an accident," Josh said. "If you'd just calm down for a minute, then I could untangle my fingers."

Chloe stopped squirming in her seat, but she continued to wail, "OOOOWWWW! OOOWWWWW!"

"She sounds like a sick cat," Robbie whispered to me.

I laughed and covered my ears with my hands.

Josh finally got his fingers free. "Sorry about that, Chloe. Like I said, it was an accident."

"But my mom just spent an hour this morning curling my hair, and now it's ruined," Chloe sniffled.

"An hour?" I whispered to Robbie. "That's crazy! I barely have time to eat breakfast. What time does she get up? Five A.M.?"

Chloe fluffed her strawberry-blond curls. "They just won't have the right bounce today," she whined.

Robbie rolled his eyes and made the cuckoo sign next to his head.

I shook my head and chuckled.

"Sorry," Josh said again.

Just then Jessie got on the bus and sat down in the seat across from us. "What's all the commotion?" she asked. "I thought I heard someone crying when I got on."

Josh silently nodded in Chloe's direction.

"Oh, gotcha," Jessie said, giving Josh a thumbs-up. "So what's happening, guys?"

"I have an RAK I can add to the chain today," I said.

"Oh, that's great!" said Jessie. "What did you do?"

"Suzie and I folded all of the laundry yesterday."

"Wait," said Robbie. "Did you say you and *Suzie*? As in, you and your sister, Suzie . . . together?

I nodded my head and grinned. "Yep."

"Holy cow! This really must be Random Acts of Kindness Week," Robbie said, laughing.

"While my mom was on the phone, the two of us folded all the laundry in the basket. When she came upstairs and saw what we had done, she was really surprised!"

"That was a great idea," said Jessie. "I also have a RAK I can add to the chain today."

"What did you do?" I asked.

"After dinner I always help my *abuela* clear the dishes from the table, but last night I also helped her wash the dishes. The dish soap made a lot of bubbles, and I got to play with them a little bit. It was a lot of fun!"

"That does sound like a lot of fun," I said. "Maybe I'll offer to help wash the dishes tonight."

"Did you guys do anything?" Jessie asked Robbie and Josh.

"My mom and I went to the grocery store after school yesterday," said Robbie. "We were waiting in line with a cart full of groceries, and then this lady came up behind us with only a carton of milk in her hand."

"I hate when that happens," said Josh. "You just have one thing, and you get stuck behind someone who has a full cart."

"I know," said Robbie. "So I asked my mom if we could let that lady go ahead of us in line. My mom thought it was a really thoughtful thing to do, so we told the lady that she could go first. She was shocked and kept thanking us over and over."

"It's crazy how such a simple thing can make people so happy," said Jessie. "How about you, Josh? Tell us what you did."

"My mom, my sister, and I went downtown yesterday because my sister needed new shoes. When we were putting money in the parking meter, I noticed that the meter next to us was expired, so that car was going to get a parking ticket. I asked my mom for an extra quarter and put it in the meter, so that person wouldn't get a ticket."

"Wow! Whoever owns that car will have no idea that you saved the day for them," I said. "That is a great RAK."

Josh smiled. "Thanks," he said.

Just then the bus pulled up at school. "Come on, guys!" Jessie said. "Let's go add our RAKs to the chain!"

As I was climbing down off the bus, I stopped and turned to Mr. Franklin. "Have a nice day!" I said.

"Thanks, Freddy! I will. And thanks again for the doughnut! It was delicious," he said, smiling and patting his stomach.

CHAPTER 5

A Fuzzy Friend

That afternoon after school, Josh, Robbie, and I had planned to go skateboarding around the neighborhood, so after they dropped their stuff off, they met me at my house.

"Hey, guys," I said as they walked up the driveway, carrying their skateboards. "I just have to grab my helmet out of the garage."

I found my helmet and put it on. "Okeydokey. Now I'm all set."

"Where do you guys want to go?" asked Robbie.

"We could go to that empty lot down the

street," said Josh. "There's a lot of space there to practice. I could teach you that new move you wanted to learn."

"Really? That would be great!" said Robbie. "I've been trying to practice it on my own, but I just can't get the hang of it. Maybe if I watch you, I can figure out what I'm doing wrong."

"Which move is that?" I asked. "The one where you spin around and do a three-sixty?"

"Yeah, that one," said Robbie. "I just can't get the board to spin fast enough."

"It's tricky, but I bet I can help you," said Josh. "Are you ready, Freddy? Come on, guys! Let's go! Race you to the end of the block."

Josh took off like a rocket. He usually beat Robbie and me because he was really good at skateboarding. He used to go to the skate park every day when he lived in California.

Robbie sailed past me, and I was struggling to keep up.

I gave myself a good push and was starting to pick up speed when all of a sudden I hit a crack in the sidewalk and lost control of my board.

"AAAAAHHHH!" I flew off my skateboard and crash-landed on Mrs. Golden's front lawn.

When Josh and Robbie realized what had happened, they came rushing back. "Freddy, are you all right?" they asked.

"Yeah, yeah, I'm fine," I said, spitting some grass out of my mouth.

"Looks like you had quite a wipeout," said Josh.

I laughed. "Yeah . . . I guess so. Good thing I was wearing this," I said, knocking on the top of my helmet. "But you know what? While I was lying here I noticed something."

"You did?" said Josh. "What did you notice? That your mouth was full of grass?"

"Ha, ha! Very funny," I said. "No, I noticed that Mrs. Golden's garden has a lot of weeds in it. Remember yesterday at school you suggested pulling weeds as a random act of kindness?"

"Oh yeah," said Josh.

"So why don't we help Mrs. Golden by pulling all the weeds out of her garden?"

"Good idea!" said Robbie.

We left our skateboards on the grass, walked over to the garden in front of Mrs. Golden's house, and got down on our knees to start pulling up all the weeds.

We had been pulling weeds for a few minutes when I said, "Hey, guys, look what I found!"

Josh and Robbie came running over.

"Look at my new fuzzy friend." A furry black caterpillar was slowly crawling up my arm. "Oooo, he tickles," I said.

"Can I have him for a minute?" said Robbie.

"Sure," I said. I gently picked him up and put him on Robbie's shirt.

The bug started crawling across Robbie's stomach. "Where did you find him?" Robbie asked.

"Right here in the dirt," I said. "He looked so cute, and he crawled right onto my finger."

"Can I have a turn?" asked Josh.

Robbie picked up the caterpillar, lifted up the bottom of Josh's shirt, and put the caterpillar on Josh's back.

"Hey! Hey! I'm going to get you for that, Robbie!" Josh squirmed and laughed. "It really is ticklish!"

Robbie and I laughed and high-fived each other.

Josh leaped up and started jumping around like a monkey.

"What's wrong?" asked Robbie. "You got ants in your pants?"

"No, I've got a caterpillar crawling up my back! Get him off! Get him off!" yelled Josh.

"All right, you little baby. I'll take him off if you stop jumping around," I said. "Stand still a minute." I took the caterpillar off Josh and put him on my head.

"You're crazy," said Josh.

"This will be a good place for him while I keep weeding," I said. "He can watch what I'm doing."

Josh shook his head and smiled. "Whatever, weirdo," he said.

The three of us continued weeding the garden. "Hey, guys, look at this," said Robbie.

Josh and I walked over to where Robbie was weeding. "Look at this trail of ants. They're all going into this anthill right here," Robbie said, pointing to a little mound of dirt.

"That is a long line of ants," I said. "It's like an ant parade."

"What's that they're carrying?" asked Josh.

"It looks like some type of dead insect," I said, putting my nose close to the line of ants so I could get a better look.

"Yeah, it looks like a grasshopper," said Robbie.

"That thing is huge," said Josh. "Way bigger and heavier than those little ants."

"Ants are amazing creatures," said Robbie. "They can actually carry up to one hundred times their body weight."

"Wow!" I said. "That *is* amazing!"

"Did you say one hundred times their weight?" said Josh.

"Yes," said Robbie. "That's like a person being able to carry a killer whale all by themselves."

"They're like little superheroes," Josh said, laughing.

I was still studying the line of ants closely when Baxter, Mrs. Golden's dog, bounded up from behind and knocked me over.

I rolled over and looked up. Baxter covered my face with wet, sloppy dog kisses. "Oh hey, boy! Thanks for cleaning my face," I said.

Mrs. Golden came trotting up the lawn. "Oh, Freddy! I am so sorry," she said. "I was taking

Baxter for a walk, and as soon as he saw you, he took off like a bolt of lightning."

I laughed. "No worries. It's fine. My face was a little dirty anyway."

"What are you boys doing here?" asked Mrs. Golden.

"We noticed that your garden had a lot of weeds in it," said Robbie.

"Oh yes! I noticed that, too," said Mrs. Golden. "I just haven't gotten around to weeding lately because I've been having a little trouble with my back."

"Well, we decided to do the weeding for you!" I said.

"Really? How sweet of you boys. What a kind thing to do!"

"All week our school is having a kindness challenge," said Josh. "We're trying to do as many random acts of kindness as we can."

"I love that idea," said Mrs. Golden. "We need a little more kindness in the world. Thank you so much, boys. I really appreciate it."

"You're welcome," we said.

"Well, one kind act deserves another in return," said Mrs. Golden. "Come on inside, boys. I've got some homemade cookies and lemonade just for you."

I rubbed my belly and smiled. Kindness really is contagious!

CHAPTER 6

Soap Bubbles

Later when my dad got home from work, my mom called, "Freddy, dinner's ready! Come to the table!"

I bounded down the stairs two at a time, raced into the kitchen, and plopped down in my chair.

"Mmmmmm . . . it smells delicious, Mom," I said, sticking my nose into my plate of spaghetti and meatballs and taking a big sniff.

"Freddy, get your face out of your plate," said my mom. "You're not a dog. You need to eat with a fork."

I picked up my fork and was about to stab a meatball when my dad grabbed my arm in midair. "Hold on there just a minute," he said.

"What's wrong?" I asked.

"Look at your hands," said my dad. "They're filthy!"

"Oh my goodness," said my mom. "They are covered in dirt. You need to go wash your hands with soap right now."

"Awwww, Mom. I'm so hungry," I said. "Can't I just start eating?"

"Not until you wash your hands," said my dad.

I jumped up from the table and ran over to the kitchen sink. I turned on the water, quickly rinsed my hands, and shook them dry. Then I started to walk back to the table.

"Hey, Freddy didn't use any soap," said Suzie.

I glared at her. "You're not the boss of me," I said.

"Look at his hands," said Suzie. "They're not even clean."

I stuck my tongue out at her when my parents weren't looking.

"With soap, Freddy," my dad said, pointing to the sink. "Go back and use the soap."

"Fine," I mumbled. I squirted a few drops of soap onto my hands and scrubbed them clean. Then I sat back down.

"Let me see your hands," said my dad. "Hold them up for inspection. I need to see the backs and the fronts."

I held up my hands for him to look at and then turned them over. My stomach grumbled. "I think my stomach is asking if it can eat now," I said.

"Yes, you may eat now," said my dad, chuckling.

I stuck my fork in my plate and started slurping up the spaghetti.

"Whoa, whoa, slow down there, Freddy," said my dad.

"You sound like a pig," said Suzie. *"SLURP . . . SLURP . . . SLURP."*

"Where are your manners?" said my mom. "Please take smaller bites, Freddy, and no slurping."

I nodded my head but kept on shoveling in the food.

"So how did your hands get so dirty?" asked my dad. "What were you doing this afternoon?"

"Well, Josh and Robbie and I were going to go skateboarding, but then we saw that Mrs. Golden had a lot of weeds in her garden. As a random act of kindness, we decided to clean up her garden for her and take out all the weeds."

"Really?" said my mom. "That was a very kind thing to do."

"We actually had a lot of fun, but my hands got dirty because I was digging in the garden."

"Was Mrs. Golden surprised?" asked my dad.

"She was out walking Baxter, and when she got back and saw what we were doing, she was really surprised!"

"I bet she was," said my mom.

"She said that she had hurt her back, so she hadn't been able to weed her garden in weeks."

"That was very thoughtful," said my dad. "I'm sure Mrs. Golden really appreciated your help."

"I just love this Random Acts of Kindness Week that your school is doing," said my mom. "It's such a great idea."

"How about you, Suzie?" asked my dad. "What did you do today?"

"Kimberly and I baked chocolate chip cookies."

"You did?" I said. "Where are they? I want one . . . or two . . . or three!"

"They're not for you," said Suzie.

I frowned. "Why not?"

"Because we made them to give away. After we finished baking, we got out our art supplies and made special cards that said things like: 'Here's a special surprise just for you' or 'A little something sweet to brighten your day.' Then we put the cookies in bags, attached one of the cards, and put them in people's mailboxes around the neighborhood."

"What a fantastic idea!" said my dad.

"I am so proud of both of you," said my mom. "You made other people very happy this afternoon."

I slurped up the last bite of my spaghetti, and then I lifted my plate up to my mouth and started to lick it clean.

"Freddy!" my mom yelled. "What are you doing?"

"Cleaning my plate," I answered while I continued to lick it.

"Put that down right now! You are not a dog. We clean plates in this house by washing them."

"Oh! That's a great idea, Mom!" I said. "Can I wash the dishes tonight?"

"You don't want to wash your hands, but you want to wash the dishes?" said my dad, shaking his head.

"Yeah. It's another random act of kindness. Mom did all the cooking, so I can wash the dishes. Do you want to help me, Suzie?" I said.

"Uh . . . sure," she said.

I picked up my plate and carried it to the sink. Suzie helped clear the rest of the dishes. Then we got to work.

"I'll wash, and then I'll pass them to you, and you can load the dishwasher," I said to Suzie.

"Okay," she said.

I turned on the faucet and filled the sink with some soapy water. I picked up the first plate and dunked it in. Some water splashed out of the sink onto Suzie's shirt.

"Hey! Watch it!" said Suzie. "We're washing dishes, not taking a bath!"

I laughed. "Here's the first one," I said, handing her the plate.

She put it in the dishwasher, and we continued this way until all the dishes were loaded.

"Is that it?" asked Suzie.

"Wait, there's one more thing," I said. I pretended to reach into the sink for another plate, but I really just stuck my hand in, grabbed some bubbles, and blew them in Suzie's direction. "Gotcha!" I said.

Suzie wiped the bubbles off her cheek, reached over, stuck *her* hand in the sink, grabbed some bubbles, and blew them at me.

Now we were in an all-out bubble war, blowing soap bubbles back and forth at each other. Before we knew it, we were covered in bubbles from head to toe.

Just then my mom walked back in the kitchen and came running over to the sink. "What in the world is going on in here?" she said.

Suzie and I laughed. "We're having a bubble war," we said.

"I thought you were washing the dishes," said my mom.

"We're all finished," I said, "so we were having a little fun."

"Well, your fun is making a big mess. Here," she said, handing us each a dish towel. "Dry yourselves off with these and wipe up the floor. Then you both need to go take a shower . . . in the actual shower, not in the kitchen sink."

CHAPTER 7

A Little Help

Wednesday and Thursday flew by because I was so busy with all my random acts of kindness. It was already Thursday night.

"Guess what, Mom?" I said as I was sitting in the kitchen, finishing up some homework.

"What, honey?"

"Tomorrow we get to see if our Kindness Chain is long enough to go around the whole school."

"That's really exciting," she said. "I wonder how many random acts of kindness will make up that chain?"

"A lot!" I said. "I bet hundreds and hundreds!"

"Freddy," said my mom. "Didn't you tell me that you are supposed to bring a book and a toy to school tomorrow to donate to the kids in the homeless shelter?"

"Oh, I almost forgot!" I said. "Thanks for reminding me, Mom. I'm done studying for my spelling test, so I'm going to go look for that stuff right now."

I went upstairs to my room and started looking through the books on my bookshelf. *Hmmm . . . let's see . . . what book am I not really reading anymore?* I thought to myself. I picked up *Arthur's New Puppy* and flipped through the pages. *I do love this one, but it's too easy for me now.* Then I saw *Don't Let the Pigeon Drive the Bus!* I pulled it off the shelf and started to read it. It was one of my favorites, too.

Suzie barged into the room.

"Get out of my room." I mumbled without looking up. "I'm busy."

"What are you doing?" she asked.

"Uh . . . if a door is closed, you're supposed to knock."

Suzie ignored what I was saying and came over to where I was sitting on the floor. "What are you reading?"

"Don't Let the Pigeon Drive the Bus!"

"Oh, I love that book!" said Suzie. "But isn't it too easy for you now?"

"Yeah, it is. Remember I said I had to bring in a book to donate to kids in the homeless shelter?"

Suzie nodded.

I held up the two books. "Well, I can't decide if I should donate *Arthur's New Puppy* or *Don't Let the Pigeon Drive the Bus!*"

"Why don't you just bring both of them in?" said Suzie. "We have so many books, and there are some kids who don't have any."

"Great idea!" I said. "I'll bring both of them to donate."

Suzie started to get up.

"Hey, wait a minute," I said, grabbing her hand. "I'm also supposed to bring in a toy. Do you want to help me pick one out?"

"Sure," said Suzie. "What were you thinking of giving away?"

"That's the problem," I said "I really don't know."

Suzie went over to my closet and opened the door. "How about your inflatable shark? You don't really play with that anymore."

"That's not true," I said. "I just took it to the pool last week. Besides, it reminds me of our trip to the aquarium."

"What about your glow-in-the-dark yo-yo?" asked Suzie. "I don't remember the last time I saw you use that thing."

"Robbie is obsessed with it. I promised I'd give it to him when I was done with it."

"I know," said Suzie, picking up a bug catcher. "How about this?

"Where did you find that?" I asked. "I've been looking everywhere for it!"

"It was right here under your baseball glove," said Suzie.

"I always leave it in the tree house. I wonder how it ended up in my closet?"

Suzie shrugged. "I have no idea, but don't you have two of these?"

"Yes, but I need both of them," I said.

"Why do you need two bug catchers?" said Suzie.

"In case I find two different kinds of bugs in one afternoon. I can't put them both in the same container. They may attack each other."

"I give up," said Suzie. "You don't like any of my suggestions." She started to walk out of my room.

"Don't go yet," I called after her. "I have to find something tonight."

Suzie paused for a minute. "I might have an idea," she said. "I'll be right back." She disappeared down the hall.

I sat down on my bed and hit my forehead with the palm of my hand—*think, think, think.*

Soon it was going to be time for bed. I had to find something fast.

Just then Suzie reappeared. "What about one of these?" she said. She was holding two board games, HiHo! Cherry-O and Candy Land. "We don't really play with either of these anymore."

I jumped off my bed and ran over to her. "Perfect!" I said. "Which one should I bring?"

"Well," said Suzie. "If you can't decide, then just bring both of them. You're bringing two books, so why not bring two games?"

I put the games and the books next to my backpack, so I wouldn't forget to take them in the morning.

"Suzie! Freddy!" my mom called. "Time to get ready for bed. It's getting late."

We brushed our teeth, put on our pajamas, and our parents tucked us in bed and kissed us good night.

I stayed awake until my parents went to bed because I had one last random act of kindness I wanted to do before tomorrow.

When the house was dark, and I was sure that everyone was asleep, I turned on my shark flashlight and pulled the small pad of sticky notes out from under my pillow where I had hidden it.

I grabbed a pen off my nightstand, and I wrote three different messages.

The first one was for Suzie. It said, "You're the best big sister in the world!"

The next one was for my dad. It said, "Thanks for teaching me how to throw a fastball!"

The last one was for my mom. It said, "You are beautiful, and you give the best hugs!"

Now came the hard part. I had to sneak out of my room in the dark and stick these in different places in the house so they would see them when they got up in the morning.

I grabbed the sticky notes and my flashlight and slowly opened my bedroom door. I peeked out. The coast was clear.

I aimed my flashlight and tiptoed to the bathroom Suzie and I share. I stuck her note on the mirror.

Then I tiptoed over to the stairs. I had to sneak downstairs without waking up my parents, which would be tricky because the second stair from the top always creaks when you step on it.

I carefully made my way down, making sure to skip the squeaky stair.

First I went into the den and stuck my dad's note on his briefcase.

Then I made my way into the kitchen and stuck my mom's note on the refrigerator. I knew she would see it there in the morning when she got up to make breakfast.

I tiptoed back through the living room and slowly climbed the stairs, once again making sure to skip the second stair from the top.

As I climbed into bed and turned off my flashlight, I smiled. My family would be so surprised when they got up tomorrow morning.

I closed my eyes and started to drift happily off to sleep . . .

Then, all of a sudden, my eyes flew open and I popped up like a jack-in-the-box. I opened my mouth and made a silent-scream face: *"AAAAHHH!"*

Tomorrow was Friday, and I still hadn't done anything nice for Max.

CHAPTER 8

Max, Max, Max

I had stayed up half the night trying to think of something nice to do for Max, so when my alarm went off the next morning, I was fast asleep. I smacked the OFF button on my clock, pulled my pillow over my head, and tried to go back to sleep.

I heard my bedroom door open. "Go away, Suzie!" I mumbled. "I'm still sleeping. Leave me alone!"

I heard footsteps getting closer to my bed.

"I said, 'Leave me alone!'" I pulled my pillow tighter over my ears.

Someone sat down on my bed. I jumped up and was about to whack Suzie with my pillow when I realized that the person on my bed wasn't Suzie. It was my mom.

I dropped the pillow. "Oh, hi, Mom," I said, yawning.

"Freddy, it's time to get up. I just came in because I wanted to thank you for the sticky note you left on the refrigerator this morning. It put a smile on my face," said my mom, and then she gave me a big hug and a kiss.

All of a sudden, Suzie and my dad appeared in the doorway. "Hey, Freddy," they said.

"Hey," I answered, and yawned another great big yawn.

"I found your note in the bathroom this morning," said Suzie. "Thanks!"

"And I found mine," said my dad. "What a nice surprise!"

I smiled, forgetting for a minute that I had no idea what I was going to do for Max.

"You must have some ninja skills," said my dad, "because I did not hear you sneaking around the house last night."

"When did you do it?" asked my mom.

"I waited until everyone was asleep, and then I tiptoed around so you guys wouldn't hear me."

"Well," said my dad. "You'd better get a move on. The bus will be here soon, and you don't want to go to school in your pajamas!"

I got dressed, brushed my teeth, and ran downstairs. I had just enough time to eat a quick bowl of cereal before the bus showed up.

I grabbed my backpack and started to run out the door. "Wait! Wait!" my mom called after me. "You almost forgot these," she said, handing me the books and the games.

"Thanks, Mom," I said. "You're right! I wouldn't want to forget them and be the only one in the class who didn't bring something in."

I sprinted to the bus and jumped on. "Good morning, Mr. Franklin," I said. "How are you today?"

"I'm great, Freddy. Just great. Thanks for asking."

I started to walk to my seat, and as I got closer to where Max was sitting, I looked down at the floor to make sure he didn't trip me.

To my surprise, his foot was not in the aisle. Maybe that was *his* random act of kindness: He wouldn't trip me today.

"Phew!" I breathed a sigh of relief as I passed

Max's seat. Then suddenly something grabbed my backpack and yanked me backwards. I fell down hard onto the floor of the bus.

I looked up and saw Max laughing hysterically. "Ha, ha, ha, ha, ha! Gotcha!" he said with a big smirk on his face.

I slowly got up and went to sit next to Josh and Robbie.

"What a jerk," said Josh.

"I don't know why he thinks that's so funny," said Robbie.

"Because he doesn't think about other people's feelings," I said.

"Hey, guys," said Jessie. "Did you remember to bring your book and toy to donate to the kids in the homeless shelter?"

"I almost forgot mine," I said, "but my mom reminded me this morning."

"What did you bring?" asked Jessie.

Josh was about to answer, but Chloe interrupted him. "I brought this Fancy Nancy book," she said, shoving the book in Jessie's face.

"There's a surprise," I whispered to Robbie.

"I wasn't asking you," said Jessie. "I was asking Josh."

"I brought the book *Put Me in the Zoo*," said Josh. "Have you ever read it?"

"Yes! Kids are going to love that one," said Jessie. "I brought *Go, Dog. Go!* It's one of my favorites."

"I love the part in that book when the dogs are wearing those crazy hats, and they ask each other, 'Do you like my hat?'" I said.

Just then Max started laughing and pointing in our direction.

"What's so funny?" said Josh.

"You are!" said Max. "You guys are such babies. I can't believe you're reading those books. I read those books when I was in kindergarten."

"We're not reading them now," said Jessie. "We brought them in to give away to kids at the homeless shelter because they are too easy for us."

"What book did *you* bring to give away?" asked Josh.

Max froze, and he got this weird look on his face.

"What's wrong?" said Jessie. "Are you too embarrassed to tell us?"

"I uh . . . I uh . . . ," Max stuttered. "I brought . . ."

"What?" said Josh. "What did you bring? *Pat the Bunny*?"

Max opened his mouth, but no words came out. Then he mumbled something we couldn't hear.

"What's that, Max?" said Josh. "What did you say? We couldn't hear you."

"I forgot," Max said.

"We still can't hear you," said Jessie.

"I forgot!" Max blurted out, and then he slumped down in his seat.

"Did he just say he forgot?" I whispered to Robbie.

Robbie nodded his head. "Yep."

"I feel kind of bad for him," I whispered. "He's probably going to be the only one who doesn't bring something in."

"Why do you feel bad for him?" said Josh. "He's always doing mean things to you."

"Freddy feels bad for him because Freddy actually cares about other people's feelings," said Jessie.

"Well, even if you do feel bad, there's nothing you can do about it now," said Josh.

"Actually, there is something I can do," I said as a big smile spread across my face.

"Why are you smiling like that?" asked Josh.

"You know how we all picked names out of a hat in our class, and we were supposed to do something kind for that person this week?"

My friends nodded.

"Well, I picked Max. And all week I haven't been able to think of a random act of kindness to do for him, but now I have."

"What do you mean?" asked Jessie.

"Last night I couldn't decide which book and which toy to bring in, so I brought two books and two toys to school today," I explained. "I could give one of my books and one of my toys to Max, so he would have something to donate."

"Well," said Jessie. "That would be a very kind thing to do."

When the bus pulled up at school, I walked over to Max's seat. "Hey, Max," I said, handing him a book and a toy. "I have this extra book and this extra toy. You can have them to bring in if you want, so you won't be the only one without something to donate."

Max stared at me for a minute without blinking. Then he said, "You would do that for me?"

I nodded.

Max took the book and the toy. "Thanks, Freddy. That's one of the nicest things anyone has ever done for me," he whispered.

"You're welcome," I said with a huge grin on my face, and then I jumped off the bus and skipped off to class.

Freddy's Fun Pages

ARE YOU READY FOR KINDNESS?

Try some of these random acts
of kindness at home, at school,
or out in your community, just like
Freddy and his friends!

At Home:

1. Clean your room without being asked.
2. Wash the dishes after a family meal.
3. Help carry in the groceries.
4. Call your grandparents to see how they are doing.
5. Write kind words for your mom, dad, brother, or sister on a sticky note and stick it up somewhere for them to see.

6. Weed the garden.

7. Read to your brother or sister.

8. Clean up a mess someone else made.

9. Draw a picture or make a gift for your brother or sister.

10. Fold the laundry.

At School:

1. Play with someone you don't usually play with at recess.

2. Help a classmate with their work.

3. Hold the door open for someone.

4. Let someone go ahead of you in line.

5. Thank an adult in the school for something they do (bus driver, cafeteria worker, front office staff, nurse).

6. Make a card for your favorite teacher.

7. Draw a picture for a friend.

8. Clean up someone else's mess.

9. Help someone carry something.

10. Pick up trash on the playground.

In Your Community:

1. Donate toys or books you don't use anymore.

2. Walk your neighbor's dog.

3. Write a kind note and leave it in someone's mailbox.

4. Rake the leaves, shovel the driveway, or mow your neighbor's lawn.

5. Pick up litter at the park or beach.

6. Write letters or send a care package to people in the military.

7. Let someone go ahead of you in line.

8. Bake cookies for the firefighters or police officers in your town.

9. Make sandwiches for a homeless shelter

10. Donate food to a food pantry.